Shabbat HICCUPS

To the PJ Library team for all of their
support and guidance—TN

For my family—IE

Library of Congress Cataloging-in-Publication data is on file with the publisher.

Text copyright © 2016 by Tracy Newman
Pictures copyright © 2016 by Albert Whitman & Company
Pictures by Ilana Exelby
Published in 2016 by Albert Whitman & Company
ISBN 978-0-8075-7312-9

Printed in China
10 9 8 7 6 5 4 3 2 1 HH 24 23 22 21 20 19 18 17 16 15

Design by Ellen Kokontis

For more information about Albert Whitman & Company,
visit our web site at www.albertwhitman.com.

Shabbat Hiccups

Tracy Newman

Pictures by
Ilana Exelby

Albert Whitman & Company
Chicago, Illinois

Every week, Jonah looked forward to Shabbat.
He loved Grandma Sue's matzoh ball soup, the warm glow of the Shabbat candles, and playing all day Saturday.

But this Friday afternoon, when Jonah set the soupspoons on the dinner table, something happened...

Jonah's cousin, Eden, tiptoed toward him, carrying the Shabbat challah.

"Boo!" she yelled.

Jonah jumped. "Whoa—what was that for?"

Eden smiled. "Just trying to scare your hiccups away before we eat."

"Oy, hiccups!" exclaimed Grandma Sue.
Mom handed Jonah a vase of flowers.
"For the table," she said.
"Pretty," said his little sister, Abby.
But all Jonah could do was...

Grandma Sue gave Jonah the sugar bowl. "Try eating some sugar. That always works for me." Jonah scooped a spoonful into his mouth. Everyone waited. Everyone was quiet. Then...

The family gathered around the table as Mom
lit candles and said the blessings.
Jonah worked hard to hold in his hiccups.

But when Dad bent down to kiss the children,
Jonah couldn't keep them in any longer—

"HICCUP!"

"HICCUP!"

"HICCUP!"

"Those hiccups don't want to go away," said
Dad. "Maybe you should try—"
"Drinking some water!" Grandma Sue
interrupted as she handed Jonah a glass.
Jonah swallowed the water in one gulp.
Everyone waited. Everyone was quiet.

"Whew!" said Jonah. "I think my hiccups are gone."
"Hooray!" everyone cheered.

On Saturday,
Jonah, Abby,
and Eden played
hide-and-seek,

built block
towers with Dad,

and listened to
Mom read a story.

When the sunlight faded, Dad opened the front door. "Let's take a walk. We can see who spots the end-of-Shabbat stars first."

Eden looked up. "The sky is getting dark."
Abby pointed. "Pink clouds."
Mom smiled. "We've had such a lovely Shabbat."
"Today has been really great," agreed Jonah.
"And I'm so happy that—

"Oh no!" wailed Jonah. "They're back."

"Oh no!" agreed Grandma Sue.

"Look," Abby tugged Grandma Sue's hand. "Three stars in the sky. Shabbat's over."

"I wish my hiccups were over too," grumbled Jonah.

"We'll get rid of them," promised Mom. "But now it's time for Havdalah."

When they got home, Jonah filled the Kiddush cup with grape juice.

Dad lit the special braided candle.

Mom said the blessing, holding the Kiddush cup high. Then she added, "Sweet juice to remember our sweet Shabbat together."

"HICCUP!"

Eden recited the blessing on the spices
and passed around a box of cinnamon sticks
and cloves.

Everyone took turns smelling the delicious scents.

"Mmmm." Dad smiled. "These spices help carry
our Shabbat memories into the week."

"Yummy," said Abby.

"HICCUP!"

Mom said the blessing over the candle, gazing at her fingertips as she held them close to the tall flame. After that, she smiled at the children and said, "A special light to brighten and warm our week."

Dad said the final blessing and drank from the Kiddush cup.

Abby, Mom, Eden, and Grandma Sue took turns drinking juice.

Grandma Sue handed the cup to Jonah. "Maybe a big sip will help get rid of those hiccups."

"I'll try," Jonah said and finished all but a few drops.

Dad poured the remaining juice into a bowl.
Mom dipped in the burning candle.

The flame hissed and sizzled and went out.
Everyone waited. Everyone was quiet.

"Woo-hoo!" Jonah exclaimed. "I think my hiccups are finally gone!"

Mom gave him a big hug. "Shavua tov."

"A good week," said Dad.

But then, something happened...

"HICCUP!"

"Oh no!" cried
Grandma Sue.
"Oh no!" agreed Jonah.
He handed Grandma
Sue a glass of water.